HAUNTED STATES
of
AMERICA

D1168893

THE DEAD
BELOW

Book design by Sarah Taplin
Cover illustration by Maggie Ivy
Interior illustrations by Eszter Szépvölgyi

Published in the United States by Jolly Fish Press, an imprint of North Star Editions, Inc.

First Edition
First Printing, 2020

This is a work of fiction. Names, characters, places, and incidents are either the product of the author's imagination or are used fictitiously, and any resemblance to actual persons living or dead, business establishments, events, or locales is entirely coincidental.

Library of Congress Cataloging-in-Publication Data
Names: Troupe, Thomas Kingsley, author.
Title: The dead below / Thomas Kingsley Troupe.
Description: First edition. | Mendota Heights, Minnesota : Jolly Fish
  Press, 2021. | Series: Haunted States of America | Audience: Grades 4-6.
  | Summary: "When Treva Gallo researches her new Philadelphia,
  Pennsylvania, neighborhood, she unearths more than she expected"—
  Provided by publisher.
Identifiers: LCCN 2020003623 (print) | LCCN 2020003624 (ebook) | ISBN
  9781631634802 (paperback) | ISBN 9781631634796 (hardcover) | ISBN
  9781631634819 (ebook)
Subjects: CYAC: Grief—Fiction. | Ghosts—Fiction. | Basketball—Fiction. |
  Moving, Household—Fiction. | Philadelphia (Pa.)—Fiction.
Classification: LCC PZ7.T7538 De 2021 (print) | LCC PZ7.T7538 (ebook) |
  DDC [Fic]—dc23
LC record available at https://lccn.loc.gov/2020003623
LC ebook record available at https://lccn.loc.gov/2020003624

Jolly Fish Press
North Star Editions, Inc.
2297 Waters Drive
Mendota Heights, MN 55120
www.jollyfishpress.com

Printed in the United States of America

HAUNTED STATES
of
AMERICA

THE DEAD
BELOW

THOMAS KINGSLEY TROUPE

JOLLY
FiSH
PRESS
Mendota Heights, Minnesota

CHAPTER 1

CHANGE OF SCENERY

Treva Gallo didn't like moving. She hadn't liked it when she was ten and her family moved to a house just outside of Philadelphia. And she didn't like it now at age fifteen, moving back to Philadelphia to an apartment in the Passyunk Square neighborhood. For one thing, the apartment was a lot smaller than her old house. For another, it was really close to the city. And most importantly, she was moving away from her friends and her basketball teammates.

She climbed the two flights of stairs to her new home with a box of books, wishing she had donated them instead of lugging them across town. Treva hip-checked the door to pop it open, and walked through the tiny apartment to her new bedroom. Being half the size of her old room, the space was already filled with moving boxes. With a grunt, she tossed the box onto

her mattress. It bounced once and turned on its side, dumping the contents across the stripped-down bed.

"Awesome," Treva muttered.

She stood for a moment and looked at what she'd already brought up from the moving truck. There were plenty more boxes where that one came from.

I need to get rid of some of my stuff, Treva thought.

There was a shuffling sound in the hallway, and she

looked to find her dad coming down the hall with two large boxes. The hallway was narrow, making it difficult for him to navigate to his room. She could hear him curse as he likely mashed his hand against a doorframe.

"You okay, Dad?" Treva asked.

The sound of boxes dropping to the ground was followed by her dad's tired exhale.

"Oh yeah," he gasped from his own bedroom. "Couldn't be better."

The floor creaked as her dad crossed the hallway to check out her room. He looked around at all of the cardboard and nodded.

"Wow," he said. "That's a lot of boxes."

"Yeah," Treva said. "Same number we loaded onto the truck."

He smirked as if he wasn't sure if she was joking or making a crack at their new place. Almost instantly, Treva felt bad.

"I was just kidding," she said. "But I really did bring too much here. I'll probably get rid of a bunch of the books I don't need anymore."

"Downsizing," Dad said. "It's not easy to do, but necessary I guess."

"I know," Treva said. "There are just some things I'm not ready to let go of yet, you know?"

Dad nodded, and Treva could see he was fighting back some tears.

"Sorry, Dad," she said, and gave him a hug. "I just miss her."

"No need to be sorry," Dad said, hugging Treva back. "I miss her too."

After a moment, they broke off the hug. She and her dad each wiped their eyes.

"Well," he said. "If we leave that truck wide open for much longer, we're not going to have anything left to move in here."

"It's not a bad neighborhood, is it?" Treva asked.

"Nah," Dad said. "Philadelphia is pretty much crime-free. They outlawed crime back in 1986."

Treva laughed and looked outside. There, parked right in front of their building, was the midsized moving truck they'd rented. The hazard lights were flashing, and the back door was wide open, exposing what they had left from their old house in Ardore.

"I think we're okay," Treva said.

"Well, I'm going to keep working," Dad announced, and left.

She heard the creak of the stairs as he made his way down to the first floor. A moment later, she peered out the window. Dad came down the front steps and headed into the truck.

"Just throw the boxes up here, and I'll catch them," Treva joked.

"Right," Dad said. "Then you can call the ambulance when my back snaps in two."

Treva took a look at the view from her bedroom window. Being on the second floor of their small brick apartment building, she could see over the trees. Spread out in front of her was a large park with a baseball diamond tucked into the right corner of the block and a soccer field marked in the grass a little farther out.

Past the soccer area, she could see two fenced-in basketball courts.

"Here we go," Treva whispered.

She watched for a moment as a group of teenagers played a pretty intense game of three-on-three. A group of older men sweated it out on the next court.

Beyond the fence and across the street was a colorful building set into the odd, triangular corner. The name JERRY'S was spelled out along the top of the building, alongside a number of signs boasting foods for sale. It took a moment for Treva to realize what the place was.

Cheesy Jerry's, Treva thought. *That's the world-famous Philly cheesesteak place.*

She'd heard of it, as it was something of a destination for foodies visiting the City of Brotherly Love, but Treva had never been there and hadn't even been sure where it was. Knowing she was going to be living that close to a relatively famous restaurant appealed to her.

It made her think the neighborhood couldn't be *that* bad.

There was a metallic squeak of shocks below, followed by her dad's voice.

"Okay, Rapunzel," he called. "You just going to stare out the window all day or are you going to help your old dad out?"

Treva snapped out of it and touched her dark, short hair.

Rapunzel?

"I'm on my way, Muscles," Treva said, and headed down.

———

After getting the last of the boxes put away and returning the moving truck to the rental place, Treva and her dad stopped at a drive-thru on the way back home and got burgers. They were both so hungry from all the hard work and exercise that they ate their food in the car.

"Excited for school?" Dad asked. He set his drink in the cupholder.

Treva gave him a look and then caught herself before he could see it.

"Not really," she said.

"C'mon," Dad said. "It won't be that bad. New start, new school . . ."

"No friends," Treva replied. "It's not easy to start tenth grade in a new school when you don't know anyone."

"I know," Dad said. "It's going to be an adjustment, but you get on the basketball team for the new school and you'll have new friends in no time."

Treva nodded. "I hope so."

"I know so," Dad said. "Trust me on this."

As they turned the corner to head down the block toward their apartment building, they passed by the bright-orange awnings on the Cheesy Jerry's building. Treva glanced at the building and noticed the place

was pretty crowded. She also saw something else as they passed.

A HELP WANTED sign.

She'd thought about getting a job before starting her sophomore year in school. It would give her something to do for the last month before school started. Plus the extra money would be nice.

"How do you feel about me getting a job?" Treva asked.

"A full-time job? You're not thinking of dropping out of school, are you?" Dad joked.

"No, no," Treva said. "Part time? Somewhere close by?"

Dad nodded as he scanned the streets for a parking spot near their building. He flipped his blinker quickly to claim his place along the curb.

"It's not the worst idea," Dad said. "It might keep you out of trouble, I suppose."

Treva snorted. Trouble was probably the last thing she'd ever gotten herself into. In her entire school career, she'd never had any sort of problem with teachers. The closest she'd gotten was getting to school a little late after a doctor's appointment in third grade. A call from Mom had cleared that right up.

Once Dad parked and they got out of the car, Treva took in their surroundings. The move to their new home in Passyunk Square felt more official to her now that their things were inside and the moving truck was long gone.

"Want to help me unpack?" Dad asked, locking up the car.

"In a little bit," Treva said. "I want to walk around a bit, if that's cool."

"Absolutely," Dad said. "Be careful, okay?"

There was a look in Dad's eye that made Treva want to cry, but she gave him a quick smile instead. It was hard enough losing one-third of the family. He wasn't about to lose any more.

"I will."

———————

Treva walked past the park, glancing through the fence at the basketball courts. There were still a bunch of teenagers playing aggressive games of three-on-three. She thought about stopping to ask them if she could play but realized she didn't have the right shorts and shoes on.

Maybe tomorrow, she thought.

She watched for a moment and listened to the smack

talk between the two teams. One of the girls, with long braids in her hair, told the girl she was guarding that she was "garbage." It was hard for Treva to tell if she really meant it or was just trying to psych out her opponent. The girl wiped her face with the bottom of her tank top. A moment later, she jumped up and smacked a shot out of the air.

"Dang, just a little competitive," Treva said to herself, and smiled.

After watching for a few more minutes, Treva walked across the street to Cheesy Jerry's. The building seemed like a frantic place with a lot going on. There were neon signs, declaring that they had the best Philly cheesesteak in the world. Another sign along the top of the building advertised that they had cheese fries too.

The place wasn't like any restaurant she'd seen before. People could eat outside at the orange picnic tables built into the sidewalk. The large orange awning wrapped around both street sides of the triangular building. Almost the entire lower floor was the kitchen, and Treva could see the cooks inside working together like a NASCAR racing team's pit crew. They slapped cheesy/meaty goodness into long bread rolls, wrapped them up, and passed them to their hungry customers.

"Hey, girl!" a voice called. "You eatin' or what?"

Treva glanced around before realizing the voice was talking to her. When she looked up, she could see a larger man with dark, greasy hair leaning forward in the order window. He was wearing a black T-shirt with a white CHEESY JERRY'S apron over it. The name tag pinned to the front said FRANK. Frank's face was glossy with sweat.

"Oh, me?"

"Yeah," Frank said. "You look hungry."

"Nah," Treva said. "I just ate, actually."

Frank shrugged and looked like he was going to turn back around to do some work in the kitchen. Before he could, Treva stepped forward.

"Hey, wait a second," she called.

"Now we're talking," Frank said. "You want a whiz with?"

Treva paused. Suddenly it felt like the guy was speaking another language.

"I'm not sure what you're—"

"The sandwich," Frank said, interrupting her. "You can get it with cheese sauce, with or without onions— that's our classic. Otherwise, we have American, provolone."

Treva shook her head. "No, no," she said. "Sorry. I'm still not hungry enough. I was wondering if I could get an application."

"A what, now?"

Treva pointed to the HELP WANTED sign.

"An application," she said. "It looks like you're hiring."

Frank laughed and shook his head.

"So you don't want to eat here, but you wanna work here?"

Treva nodded. "Oh, I'm sure I'll eat here at some—"

"Hey, kid," Frank said. "I'm busting your chops, just messing around. Let me go grab Ronny. He'll talk to you."

Before Treva could respond, Frank leaned back from the window and hollered toward the back of the kitchen to someone she couldn't see. As he did, the other cooks in the kitchen glanced over to give Treva a quick glance.

This place is something else, she thought.

A moment later an older guy with white, styled hair poked his head out through the window.

"Yeah?" he asked Treva. "What do you need?"

Not a single word passed her lips before Frank jumped in.

"She's looking for a job, Ronny," he said.

Ronny turned to look at Frank and then back at Treva.

"Oh yeah? A job?" Ronny asked. "Is that so?"

Treva nodded but wondered if she actually wanted to work with a couple of odd guys like Ronny and Frank.

"Why do you want to work here?" Ronny's eyes narrowed as if he were trying to determine if she was hiding something from him.

"Well," Treva said. "I live close, over on 10th Street, and I figured . . ."

"Fine," Ronny said. "You're hired. You can start tomorrow afternoon."

Treva was stunned. No application, no interview. Just like that, she had a job.

"There you go, kid," Frank said. "Guess we'll see you tomorrow at one."

It wasn't until after she left that she realized they hadn't even asked her name.

CHAPTER 2

HOLDING COURT

Treva unlocked the door to their apartment, excited to tell her dad the news. When she opened the door, she noticed it was oddly quiet, especially for a guy who was bound and determined to get unpacked as soon as possible.

"Dad?" Treva called. "Are you here?"

She closed the door behind her, cutting off the odd smell of burning microwave popcorn that emanated from the hallway. With a quick twist, she locked the door and listened for any sort of response or movement. It was still eerily quiet.

"Dad?"

Treva walked to the small window in the apartment's living room and glanced outside. Their car was still parked out front. She knew he was still there, unless he'd decided to walk around the neighborhood too.

She turned and saw a number of flattened cardboard boxes stacked near the kitchen counter. Through the glass on the cupboard doors, Treva saw that the familiar plates and bowls had already found their new home.

Dad has been busy unpacking, she thought. *But where is he?*

Considering the apartment wasn't exactly huge, Treva knew she'd find him sooner or later. She walked down the hall where their bedrooms and the single bathroom were located. The bathroom was open, and a small box sat in the middle of the floor. She continued down the hall and peered into her dad's bedroom.

Lying on his back, sound asleep in the sweaty T-shirt and shorts he'd been wearing all day, was her dad. His round belly rose and fell with every breath, his mouth emitting a small snore each time. He held a pair of balled-up socks in his left hand as if he'd been working to put his clothes away and just dropped right to sleep.

Wiped out, Treva thought, and smiled.

Treva glanced at the digital clock on his nightstand. It was plugged in, but it flashed the time 12:00 a.m. over and over in bright-red lights. She pulled her phone out of her pocket and checked the time. It was just before 8:00 p.m.

Not having the heart to wake him up, Treva turned

off the light and slowly closed his door, wincing when the hinge squeaked the tiniest bit.

She went into her own room and stopped to look at the piles of boxes she had to unpack. Treva wasn't sure if she was expecting all of her stuff to magically find its place in her new space, but it didn't happen. Knowing she would likely never fall asleep surrounded by cardboard, Treva went to work on putting her new room together.

———————

At breakfast the next morning, Treva shared the big news with her dad.

"So, I got a job yesterday," she said.

Treva dunked some of her dry chocolate cereal under the milk in her bowl.

"You're kidding me," Dad said. His face hovered over his steaming mug of coffee. "Where?"

Treva nodded toward their living room window.

"That cheesesteak place," she replied.

"Which one?"

Treva looked confused.

"There's two of them within a block of each other," Dad said. "Queen of Steaks and Cheesy Jerry's."

"Oh, crazy," Treva replied. "I didn't know that. The cheesy one hired me. We drove by it last night."

Dad nodded. "Well, that was quick," he said. "What're they going to have you do?"

Treva shrugged as she ate a spoonful of cereal. "Not sure. Maybe stuff in the kitchen or whatever?"

Dad set his coffee down.

"You didn't find out what your job duties will be?"

"I guess not," Treva admitted. "Was I supposed to?"

"Usually that's how it goes," Dad replied. "Who hired you?"

"The owner of the place, I think," Treva said. She felt like her big news wasn't landing as she'd expected with her dad. "It's weird. I asked for an application and they just pretty much hired me on the spot."

Dad shook his head. "This seems kind of fishy to me," he said. "I'm not quite sure I like it."

"Do you want me to tell them I can't work there?" Treva asked. "I'm sure I can get a job somewhere else. I just thought it was a good place, since it's barely a block away."

Her dad was quiet for a minute. She could see he was torn somehow, as if unsure what the right way to go was.

"When are you supposed to start?" Dad asked.

"One p.m. today."

"Okay, I'll go over there with you," Dad said.

"Seriously?"

"Yeah," Dad said. "I want to make sure these guys are on the level. Introduce myself, all of that. You know?"

"You're totally going to embarrass me," Treva said. "I think I'd rather quit and get a different job."

"Give your old man some credit," Dad said, pretending to look hurt. "When have I ever embarrassed you?"

Treva's eyes widened but she kept her mouth shut.

"Maybe they just do things a little differently in the city," Dad said. "We'll get it squared away."

"Okay, fine," Treva said.

She stood up and picked up her cereal bowl, brought it to the sink, and dumped the little bit of chocolate milk down the drain.

"What're your plans before work?" Dad asked. "Going to unpack?"

Treva turned and smiled. "Nope," she said. "Already done. I'm going to go across the street and shoot some hoops. Don't want to lose my killer jump shot."

Dad nodded.

"Good plan, good plan," he said. "Your new school will be lucky to have you on the team."

———————

Treva dribbled twice on the cracked pavement on court two in Capitolo Playground and put up a shot. The ball slammed against the metal backboard, dropped, and went wild to the left. She scrambled to grab it before it went out of bounds, dribbled, spun, and shot again. The ball went over the hoop without even touching it.

Air ball, Treva thought. *I need to sharpen my skills, or I'll be watching the games from the stands.*

She hustled after the ball again. It was just last year that she'd gotten the most rebounds for her team, making her a huge asset on both offense and defense. When she recovered the ball, she paused to look around the park a bit. There were murals of children's faces painted on the sides of the park buildings. A group of young soccer players was gathering on the fields, kicking balls back and forth across the dewy grass.

Two little kids were squealing as they chased each other around the new play structure while their mom stared at her smartphone.

Treva was alone on the court, dribbling and moving the ball between her legs without any effort. She glanced

through the chain-link fence and could see some of the people inside Cheesy Jerry's moving around inside the kitchen.

Doesn't that place ever close? she wondered, then glanced at the neon sign she hadn't noticed before: OPEN 24 HOURS.

Guess not. But who's eating a cheesesteak sandwich at 9:30 a.m.?

Treva put up another shot and watched it bounce on the backboard, hit the front of the rim, and then tip back enough to drop through the hoop. Instead of celebrating her victorious first basket, she dashed forward, grabbed the ball, and dribbled to the free throw line.

As she lined up her shot, Treva saw two guys and a girl around her age coming up the sidewalk. They had a basketball and were dribbling it along the way, laughing together.

She shot from the free throw line, hoping it would drop through the hoop. Thankfully, it did, but even so, Treva pretended like she didn't care if the approaching basketball players noticed it.

The group walked over to the court next to Treva's and began to play. She glanced over at them periodically, as if willing them to ask her to come and get a game of two-on-two going. As she continued to practice and work on her form, another group of four headed toward the next-door court. She recognized one of the girls from yesterday. It was the girl with the braids and the big mouth.

"You all out here to ruin your morning?" the girl shouted. She smiled wide as if to show everyone she was just playing around. "Another day, another L for the books? Is that what we're thinking?"

Even though she was talking smack, the first group greeted her.

"Your chattering big mouth is enough to ruin an entire day, Des," a boy in a backward ball cap said.

There were *ooohs* from the opposing team and a couple of laughs. The girl, Des, wasn't about to be outdone. She snapped right back.

"When you've got the skills to back it up, you can talk as much as you want," Des said. "Until then? Keep quiet, Carlos."

She pretended to wipe dust from her shoulders as if she wasn't even affected by his comeback.

"So, what's up?" a guy from Des's team said. "Are we playing or not? You guys look a little short."

"Yeah," another boy from the first group said.

"Jay isn't coming. He's grounded until next year or something."

"Great," Des said, clearly upset.

There was a pause, and Treva felt all seven pairs of eyes look her way. She dribbled once and fired off a jump shot.

Make it, make it, make it, she thought as the ball was airborne.

The ball hit a perfect arc and dropped through the netless hoop without ever touching the edges.

Swish.

She grabbed the ball without even looking at the others on the neighboring court.

There was mumbling from the group, and Treva dribbled back to the top of the key, pretending not to care what the neighborhood players were talking about.

"I don't really care," she heard Des mumble. "I just want to play."

Carlos, the boy in the backward cap, called over to her.

"Hey," he shouted.

Treva stopped and looked over as if she'd been concentrating on her ballhandling. She even pointed at herself and gave them a look.

Who, me?

"We're short over here and wondered if you wanted to play with us," the boy said. "Four-on-four?"

Treva took a deep breath and nodded.

"Yeah, sure," Treva said. "Okay."

"That's three yeses," Des said with a smirk. "I think the new girl is in."

Treva dribbled over to the neighboring court and introduced herself. Carlos introduced the other girl as Hailey. The quiet guy on her team was Tim.

"Sorry to say it, but you're going to have to cover Des," Carlos said.

"Yeah, sorry about that," Des said. "You're not going to like it."

Treva smirked. "Oh, I'm sure I'll be just fine."

The game was frantic and a little more aggressive than any Treva had played before. Since there was no referee, there were more shoving and wild shots than she was used to. Des proved to be a formidable opponent, almost effortlessly driving to the basket, turning, and making incredible shots, even when Treva was on top of her.

"Nice shot," Treva said after Des increased her team's lead by eight.

"Nice doesn't even come close," Des said with a nasty wink.

Treva held her own. She turned at the last second anytime Des tried to steal the ball. She pump-faked, making Des jump prematurely before taking the shot. Though Treva was fine sharing the spotlight with the rest of her team, she took some pride in getting Des to keep quiet, even if it were only for a moment at a time.

After a while, they took a break. Carlos pulled off his cap, wiped the sweat off his forehead, and pulled his dark hair back to reapply his hat.

"You're pretty good, Tina," he said.

"Treva," she said, correcting him. "And thanks."

"Sorry," he said. "Treva."

"Jay can stay grounded," Hailey said. "He's sloppy compared to you."

Treva smiled.

"It doesn't matter who you bring," Des said. "Jay, this new girl, or LeBron James. It still isn't enough to take us down."

"Ignore her," Carlos said. "She's all talk. We beat her once."

"When was that?" Treva asked.

"Last summer," Hailey replied. "But hey, I think you've got her worried."

Treva laughed. As cliché as it sounded, she didn't really care if they won or lost. She was just happy to be playing. Practice was practice, and it was only going to help her get onto her new school's team.

She raised her arms to stretch and looked around. She noticed a man standing by the park building near the wall with the painted faces. The man was dressed in long, dark pants, a grayish shirt, and a suit coat. He stared back at Treva with what looked like dark eyes.

It was too far to see, but it looked like the man hadn't slept in days.

What's his deal? Treva thought, stopping midstretch to watch him for a moment.

The man didn't move but kept staring. Treva stared right back and realized he looked different, almost faded, somehow. She shook her head and drew her gaze away. *Why does he seem blurry? Do I need to get my eyes checked?*

She turned to see Des watching her with dissecting eyes.

"What are you looking at, New Girl?"

Treva wasn't sure if Des was truly asking or just being aggressive. Without replying, she looked back to where she'd spotted the strange man.

He was gone, almost as if he'd disappeared or was never there in the first place.

"Nothing, I guess," Treva whispered.

CHAPTER 3

FIRST SHIFT

Treva and the neighborhood kids played a handful of games, each one more intense than the last. Try as they might, Treva's team wasn't able to beat Des's group. Des made sure to let them know how much they stunk and added that even trying to beat her and her squad was a waste of time.

"Leave that weak stuff at home," Des shouted.

"You beat us by two points," Treva said. "Not sure I'd be bragging."

"Still a win, New Girl," Des said, making a *W* with her hands. "Still a win."

Carlos pulled Treva aside.

"Don't let her get to you," he said. "She's never had anyone make her work as hard as you do. I think you've got her worried. She treats talking smack like it's her job."

Job, Treva thought. She glanced across the street at the site of her own job.

Treva snapped up her phone from the grass and touched the screen. It was 12:33 p.m.

Though they were done playing for the day, Treva called out to her team.

"Hey, I have to go," she said. "But let's do this again!"

Her team nodded and waved to her, but Des couldn't help but get in the last word.

"Yeah, come by anytime you want to get your butt kicked, New Girl!"

Treva took a deep breath and bit her tongue. She had about thirteen comebacks for Des's smart mouth but kept them to herself.

Feeling good but rushed, Treva collected her ball and headed across the fields and back home.

———

After a quick shower and a change of clothes, Treva grabbed her keys and phone from the kitchen counter.

"Ready to go?" Dad called from the couch in the living room.

I was hoping he'd forgotten about this, she thought.

"Dad," she said, almost pleading. "You don't need to do this. I'm going to be fine."

"Yeah, but I'm your dad," he said. "And I sort of need to make sure."

He stood up and stretched. Treva heard his back pop, and he groaned, cracking his knuckles over his head as if preparing for some sort of scuffle.

"Well, just don't say anything embarrassing," Treva said. "Please. I'm going to have to work with these guys, and I'd rather not get off on the wrong foot."

Dad smirked. "No promises," he said.

The two of them walked down 10th Street and turned right on Federal, walking past the park. As they did, Treva was relieved that her new basketball friends and Des were nowhere to be seen. She suddenly didn't like the idea of them playing without her.

"How did you look out there?" Dad asked, noticing Treva watching the courts.

"Pretty good, I guess," Treva said. "It's different playing in the park when you're used to being in the gym."

Dad nodded. "Some of the best undiscovered players are out in the parks around the country," he said. "There are players out there that could give the pros a run for their money."

"I bet you're right," Treva said. She wondered if a talent scout might swing by one of their games someday. Maybe they'd pick her instead of Des.

Des would lose it if THAT happened.

HAUNTED STATES OF AMERICA

After a few minutes, they arrived at Cheesy Jerry's. As soon as they got within earshot, Frank shouted out to the two of them.

"Hey, what're you two eating?"

A knot instantly formed in Treva's stomach. *Did they already forget they hired me?*

She realized that Frank probably saw thousands of people every week. There was no way for him to remember every face that happened along their sidewalk.

"It's me," Treva said with a quick wave. "Treva."

"Oh, right," Frank said. "The new girl. Your name is Treva?"

She could feel her dad staring at the side of her head.

Oh wow, this is not off to a good start, she thought.

"Yes," Treva said. "This is my dad, Paul. He wanted to make sure you guys had actually hired me."

Frank turned and looked at Paul Gallo. He scrunched up his mouth as if he didn't know what to make of the situation. Before Frank could say anything, her dad piped up.

"Are you the manager here?"

"Nah, nah," Frank said. "Let me get him, though."

After a moment of shouting through the kitchen,

Ronny poked his head through the window too. Treva watched as the three men introduced themselves while she stood there feeling like a child.

"So she said you guys hired her, no interview, no application or anything," her dad said.

"Yeah, well," Ronny said, glancing at Treva. "We get a lot of kids who want a job with us. They fill out the application, we talk with them, and then they never show up for work. It wastes a lot of time, and as you can see . . ." Ronny gestured to the lines queued up along both sides of the building.

"You guys are really busy," Dad said. "I get that."

"The way I figure it," Ronny said, "your kid showed initiative and dependability by walking up to ask for a job and actually showing up when I told her to. In my eyes, she passed the most important part of working here at CJ's. Reliability."

Treva smiled and could tell by her dad's reaction that he liked these guys.

"We're a family-run business, Paulie," Ronny said. "And even if you're not in our actual family, we treat everyone who works here like they are."

"That's great," Dad said. "As a single dad, I just want to make sure Treva is going to be okay working here."

"Hey, I get it, buddy," Ronny said. "My own daughter's first job was here, and she still puts in a shift every now and again. We might seem like a bunch of goofballs, but we're good guys, and we'll make sure she's treated right."

Treva and Ronny worked out her schedule, pay, and expectations while her dad "supervised." She quickly learned that she could only work three hours on school days and up to eight hours on non-school days. The state law wouldn't let her work later than 7:00 p.m. The best part? Ronny was fine with her picking how long she wanted to work each day.

"We'll always have jobs for her to do around here," Ronny said.

"Sounds great," Dad said, glancing over at Treva. "Well, hey, that's all I needed to hear."

"Good," Treva said, feeling like they'd been standing there too long.

"If anything comes up, we're just across the park," Dad said, pointing to their brick apartment building. "I can keep an eye on her from there."

Oh, c'mon, Treva thought.

"Thanks, Dad," she said quickly. "Got to get to work now. Bye."

After a quick hug from her dad, who got waves from

both Ronny and Frank, Treva was finally ready to start her first day of work.

———————

Frank opened up the side door and gave her a quick tour of the building, showing her where the supplies were kept, where she'd clock in and out, and what each station in the kitchen did. While she could smell the grilled meat and onions from the sidewalk, the aroma was almost overpowering when she was up close.

"You'll get used to the smell in here after a while," Frank promised. "But the good news? A good chunk of your job will be outside, on the sidewalk."

"What?" Treva asked.

"Yeah," he said. "As you can probably see, we don't have a dining room or anything. All of our customers are pretty much to go, unless you get some people who just can't wait. They stick around and eat on the picnic tables."

"Oh, okay," Treva replied.

"You're going to be our captain of first impressions," Frank said. "Help us keep the area cleaned up, you know? Wipe the picnic tables, sweep up a bit, maybe empty a trash can or two."

"Yeah, no problem," Treva said.

"We'll also need you to get us stuff from the back when we're running low," Frank said. "We might need rolls, cheese, onions, paper wraps, that kind of thing. Keep making us look good and we'll move you into the kitchen, where the real magic happens."

Treva nodded. She wasn't sure she really aspired to be a cook at Cheesy Jerry's but appreciated Frank's enthusiasm.

He showed her the rest of the place, including a small area behind the kitchen. There, Treva saw a corner booth, surrounded by framed photos of famous people.

"Whoa, what's this?" Treva asked.

"This is where we bring celebrities that want to stop by for one of our famous sandwiches," Frank explained. "This gets them away from gawkers and people bothering them for autographs."

Treva looked at the pictures and recognized a number of people from movies and TV shows that she liked.

"Okay, here's your uniform," Frank said, handing her a Cheesy Jerry's T-shirt and an apron. "Welcome to the team, T."

———

That afternoon, Treva wiped countless picnic tables and swept stray papers and bits of food from the

sidewalk. She made sure the bright-orange trash barrels weren't overflowing and kept the condiment and napkin dispensers full. It wasn't the most glamorous job, but she didn't care. Other than the basketball crew she'd met at Capitolo earlier, she didn't know anyone else.

The crowds were steady for the midafternoon, making Treva realize that Cheesy Jerry's really was something of a tourist destination. People walked up and seemed to be speaking another language as they ordered "whiz with" or "American without." When customers were confused, they were given a quick lesson from the guys in the kitchen on how to order properly.

As Treva swept the sidewalk on the right side of the building, she noticed a small family enjoying a late lunch. Two men and a little girl were eating their sandwiches. At the end of the table was an older woman dressed in a long black dress. She wore a large veiled black hat that partially covered her face. She seemed like she didn't belong, dressed as she was. The woman appeared disconnected from the others eating at her table, almost like she'd joined a group of strangers. There was nothing in front of her to eat, but she stared at the table as if waiting or hoping for someone to bring her something.

Treva caught herself staring and shook it off, continuing to sweep and make sure the exterior of CJ's was running smoothly.

As she got near the table, the old woman reached out toward her as if she meant to grab Treva's arm. Startled, Treva scrambled backward, knocked into a customer, and made him drop his sandwich. She stumbled a little and fell down hard on her backside.

"Hey," the middle-aged man cried. "Are you okay?"

The two men and the little girl at the table turned to look at her too. Treva blinked a few times before nodding. She let the man help her to her feet before

he retrieved his sandwich from the ground. He also handed her the broom she was holding.

"I'm so sorry," Treva gasped, feeling her cheeks flush hot with embarrassment. "I can have the guys get you another—"

"No need," the guy said. "The sandwich is fine. Still wrapped up. I'm just glad you aren't hurt."

"Yeah," Treva said. "Thanks, I'm okay. I just . . ."

She turned to look at the old woman who had reached out to grab her. The spot on the bench where she'd been sitting was empty. The men and the little girl at the table watched her, as if wondering what she was looking at. Treva looked up and down the sidewalk.

"Tripped, I guess," she finished. The old woman, whoever she was, was gone.

CHAPTER 4

SECOND SIGHT

Treva was prepared to walk down the block, looking for the old woman, but decided against it. It was almost the end of her shift, and walking away from her job on the first day seemed like a pretty bad move.

I'm just seeing things, she reasoned. *It's hot out, and there are a lot of people around.*

Even so, she couldn't shake the image of the old woman. Anytime she held her eyes closed for longer than a moment, she could see her . . . just as she had briefly seen her the first time. The woman's skin had been ashen and lined with wrinkles. Her cheeks had hung slack on her face, as if age and gravity had caught up to her.

Treva had been startled, worried that the woman was trying to grab or startle her somehow. The more she thought about it, the less she thought that was the case. The old woman's face seemed desperate and sad, not threatening. It was almost like she was trying to get Treva's attention, not scare her.

But who was she? Treva thought, pulling a full garbage bag out of one of the containers. *And what did she want?*

At the end of her shift, she went back inside to clock out for the day. Frank came over, wiping his hands on the front of his apron. He smelled like grilled onions.

"How'd the first day go, T?"

Treva tried to push her "accident" out of her mind but wasn't sure if the guys inside had seen what happened.

"Pretty good," she replied. "Up until I got startled and knocked a sandwich out of a customer's hand. He didn't seem upset or anything, so I guess that's good?"

"Well, if he was really mad about it, we would've made it right," Frank said with a quick shrug. "Accidents happen, am I right?"

"Absolutely," Treva said. "You guys want me back tomorrow?"

Frank walked over to the schedule pinned up near the time clock. He traced his finger along a column of dates and names and nodded his head.

"Yeah, let's have you back tomorrow, but if you want to come in Monday too, that would be swell, T."

Treva nodded, pulled her phone out of her pocket, and updated her calendar.

"You got it," she said. "I'll be here."

"Great," Frank said. "We're glad to have you aboard. Hey, you want a sandwich for the road?"

———————

The walk back to her house took less than five minutes, but as she passed Capitolo Playground, she couldn't help but want to get back out there and play a game with Carlos and his team. She was even willing to play one-on-one with Des if the opportunity presented itself.

Instead, she could only see a group of college-aged boys roughhousing their way through a pretty brutal game of two-on-two. She wasn't sure they'd want her to play, and she definitely didn't want to catch an elbow in the teeth.

Inside her building, she climbed the steps to the second floor and turned right to head toward her apartment. Standing at the end of the hallway was the silhouette of a young woman. The light coming from the window behind her made her look mostly like a shadow, obscuring her features.

"Hello," Treva said, thinking it must be one of their neighbors.

The figure at the end of the hallway didn't respond. She just stood silent. Her nearly hidden facial features seemed to be staring at Treva, watching her.

Okay, Treva thought. *Time to get inside.*

She felt her heart pick up speed as she fumbled for her keys. As she walked toward the woman to get to her door, the figure shifted slightly and then walked to the left, as if ducking into her own apartment. In moments, she was gone.

With her key partway into the lock, Treva glanced up. She looked at where the woman had gone. There wasn't a door at the very end of the hallway. Just a wall, a radiator, and a metal box containing a fire extinguisher.

"Seriously," Treva whispered. "What is happening?"

She stood still for a moment, watching the end of the hallway, where the shadowy figure had stood just moments before. The apartments on the second floor were mostly quiet, except for the dull drone of a TV inside the unit across the hall.

Treva took a step forward, almost afraid to blink, in case the woman appeared again. As she got closer, she could feel the temperature drop a bit with every step. In a matter of moments, she stood in front of the dirty double-hung window that offered a view of the brick apartment building next door.

There was no trace of the woman she'd seen. Looking to her left and right confirmed there were no doors she could have escaped through. The area was just oddly cold.

A door opened suddenly, and Treva cried out.

"Pardon me," a scratchy voice said.

She turned from the window to see an older man sporting a bathrobe and insanely bushy, white eyebrows. He glanced at her for a moment before he shuffled down the hall to the stairs, a set of keys jangling in his large, wrinkled hand.

Great, Treva thought. *Making a memorable first impression on the neighbors.*

Her heart thrummed, and her face felt hot with embarrassment, almost overshadowing her thoughts about the strange woman she'd seen.

She walked back to the door to apartment 204, slid her key into the lock, and glanced down the hallway one last time, almost expecting to see the shadowy figure watching her from afar again.

There was nothing except the sun sneaking in through the window and silence.

———————

After everything that had happened, Treva didn't feel like eating. In the space of seven hours or so, she'd seen three things she couldn't explain that creeped her out: the man in the park, the old woman at Cheesy Jerry's, and the shadow in the hallway.

She put the Cheesy Jerry's sandwich in the refrigerator and found the note on the counter from her dad.

Had to run to work for a bit tonight. Hope your first day went well! Go ahead and eat without me! See you soon. Love, Dad

Treva smiled. In an age of smartphones and text messages, her dad still liked to leave handwritten messages. He said it reminded him of when he was a kid and it was almost like getting a letter in the mail. *A text message is disposable, forgettable,* he'd said once.

She walked through the apartment, weaving her way through the few boxes that still needed to be unpacked. It looked like he'd been busy while she'd been at work. There were even more empty, flattened boxes that needed to find their way to the recycling bin behind the building.

Treva sat on the couch and picked up the remote for the TV. She pushed the power button and nothing happened. A quick look along the wall showed her the television hadn't been plugged in yet. Not sure she wanted to watch anything anyway, she tossed the remote down and glanced out the window.

A group of people was standing near the basketball courts. They looked to be about Treva's age. In an effort to take her mind off the weirdness of the day, she went to her room, changed, and found her basketball.

As she headed out, she stopped at the counter. Treva flipped Dad's note over and scrawled a quick message to him.

Dad, I'm at the park playing basketball. Sorry you had to work! Maybe that sandwich I left for you in the fridge will help! I'll be back before dark. Love, T

———————

"Well, look who's here," someone called from behind Treva.

Even though she'd only met her once, it didn't take a genius to figure out who the voice belonged to. She turned to confirm and offered up the best smile she could manage.

Des stood at the edge of the court, a red-and-black basketball in the nook of her left arm.

"I heard you were going to be here," Treva said. "So I came running."

Des smirked, though it looked like it pained her to do it.

"Very funny, New Girl," Des replied.

The two of them were silent, watching the college guys hotdog and bad-mouth each other on the court. A group of six had already started a game next to them and didn't seem like they were too interested in switching or adding players just yet.

"That guy is a straight-up ball hog," Des mumbled, mostly to herself.

Treva looked and saw who she was talking about. A guy in enormous black-and-gray camouflage shorts was ignoring his teammates. Even though they waved and hooted to get his attention and let him know they were wide open.

Yeah, Treva thought. *You'd NEVER do anything like that, would you, Des?*

The two of them watched the others play for a while, not really saying anything. Treva bounced her ball a few times, as if to signal to the other games that they were waiting or willing to jump in if needed. As she did, she glanced up at Des, who was staring off toward the mostly empty soccer fields.

Treva followed her gaze. Standing in the middle of the mashed grass were three solemn-looking teenagers, watching them from afar. All three of them looked out of place. The boys were dressed in pants and button-down shirts. The girl wore an old-fashioned dress that looked like she was going to a fancy ball or funeral.

Treva noticed the three outsiders seemed faded,

almost distorted in appearance. Within moments, the entire group disappeared, until the soccer field was empty again.

Treva heard Des take a deep breath. "Well," Des said. "This is pointless. I'm getting out of here." Then she started to head toward the opening in the fence.

Treva felt a surge of excitement rise up in her chest. *She can't leave yet!* No one else had seemed to notice the trio of teenagers disappear into thin air. *No one, that is . . . except Des.*

CHAPTER 5

NOT ALONE

Des made to leave, but Treva stood there stunned.

What in the world just happened?

"Hey!" Treva called to Des. "Wait up!"

Des kept walking down the street as if she didn't hear a thing. She glanced quickly over at the soccer fields through the fence, then glanced back. It was just enough time for Treva to see that she wasn't just being rude as usual but had earbuds in.

Treva ran after Des and, when she reached her, tapped her on the shoulder. Des jumped and spun around, raising her fist as if she was ready to use it.

"Whoa, whoa," Treva said, taking a step back.

"Oh, c'mon," Des said. "You can't do that to someone, New Girl! I almost knocked your teeth in!"

Treva held up her hands and smiled sheepishly. After a moment, Des took her earbuds out and tucked them into her shorts pocket.

"You trying to follow me home?"

"No," Treva said. "I just wanted to talk to you for a second."

Des raised an eyebrow and nodded toward the park. "We were standing there for like a half hour. You couldn't talk to me then?"

Treva sighed.

"I'm Treva Gallo," she said. "And I wanted to ask you something without everyone else around."

Des narrowed her eyes for a moment, then softened.

"Destiny Williams," Des said. "And just so you know, no one but my grandma calls me that."

"Fair enough," Treva said.

Treva paused a moment and then nodded toward the soccer field. "You saw them too, didn't you?" she asked quietly.

Des suddenly looked like someone had knocked the wind out of her. She shook her head a bit and glanced around as if worried others might hear the two of them.

"I don't know what you're talking about, New Girl," Des whispered.

Treva pointed to the soccer fields and then to the park building with the painted face murals on the side.

"Those people standing in the soccer field," Treva whispered back. "You caught me looking at the guy yesterday during the game. Today I caught you looking at the people out in the middle of the field. One minute they were there, the next they were gone."

Des took a deep breath and held it in. To Treva, she looked like a time bomb ready to explode at any second. Even so, she stayed silent.

"What's going on around here?" Treva asked.

Des let out her breath. "I didn't see anything, okay?"

she said. "It's just your imagination. I don't know what's wrong with you, acting like seeing some kids out in the field is—"

Treva's face lit up. "I never said they were kids! I knew you saw them!"

Des exhaled and looked across the street at the Mexican restaurant next to Cheesy Jerry's.

Treva continued, "They looked like people from an old photograph or something, like time travelers or—"

"Look," Des warned. "You need to get out of my face with this nonsense, do you understand? Just because you're seeing things, doesn't mean I am too."

Treva put up her hands to show she wasn't going to push anymore.

"I'm sorry," Treva said. "I'm not trying to make you mad. But in the past day, I've seen half a dozen people I can't explain. It's only since I've moved here, but they keep showing up."

"Yeah?" Des said with a nod. "Then you'd best ignore them, New Girl." She grabbed her earbuds to put them back in. "Because if you don't? They'll never leave you alone."

And with that, Destiny Williams left Treva standing on the sidewalk, even more confused than she was before. Behind her, Treva could hear the squeak of shoes on the concrete and the murmurs of players calling plays to each other.

——————

Treva tapped the metal base of her bedside lamp that evening, turning it on. She'd loved the lamp ever since she'd first seen it a few years ago. She wished there was enough space in her bedroom to put one on the other side of her bed. She tapped it twice more to make the light as bright as possible.

She'd spent the evening trying to keep her mind occupied and unpacked as much of the living room as she could. Treva had set up the television and talked with her dad while he ate the sandwich she'd brought from work as a late dinner.

Now that it was coming up on midnight and Dad was asleep, their small apartment was silent. Without warning, her mind went back to the people she'd seen disappear before her eyes.

What were they? Hallucinations?

That didn't make sense. If it truly was her mind playing tricks on her, why was Des seeing them too? Though her basketball rival wouldn't admit it, there was no doubt in Treva's mind that Des had spotted the strange visitors in the park.

Treva stood near her open window, looking out across 10th Street and beyond. The road was illuminated with lamps, and there were a few lights near the building in Capitolo Playground. Even farther out she could see the bright neon from Cheesy Jerry's, open and serving hungry customers around the clock.

The streets were quiet, with only the occasional car making its way through the neighborhood, headlights momentarily cutting through the dark. There didn't seem to be anyone walking around out there, making Treva think pretty much the rest of the neighborhood was asleep. A light breeze made her curtains flap a bit on either side of the window pane.

And then, she saw someone strange.

An old man was standing near the edge of the baseball diamond. He had one foot in the sand and the other in the dark grass. Though the distance and darkness made it difficult to tell for sure, it looked like he was wearing a shabby, dark suit. His face looked empty and expressionless, as if he was disoriented or lost.

Treva watched as the man tilted his head up to look her way.

Realizing she was completely illuminated in her bedroom window, she ducked and tapped the base of her lamp, killing the light. Her room was quickly flooded with darkness, but the image of the man was stuck in her head. Very slowly, she lifted her head up to peek out the window.

The man was still there, staring up at her apartment building.

"Can he see me?" Treva whispered. Her blood screamed through her veins as her heart raced.

A moment later, the man walked forward toward her building. She watched in shock as he slowly crossed the baseball diamond. The old man moved slowly toward the fence. Then he passed through it as if it didn't exist.

What is happening? Treva's mind screamed.

She strained her eyes, forcing herself not to blink. The man walked onto the sidewalk, glanced down each side of the street, and then fixed his eyes on the apartment again.

I'm not hallucinating, she realized. *He's a ghost. I'm seeing ghosts!*

Treva shuddered as she watched the ghost step to the left before turning and walking the other way. When her eyes couldn't stand it anymore, she blinked, giving them a moment of relief. She opened them again to see the old man start to fade away into nothing near a minivan parked along the curb.

Thinking the man was gone and feeling a little braver than she had a moment ago, Treva stood up. She gazed out the window, scanning the sidewalk and the park for him. There was no trace of him anywhere—or any other mysterious figures either.

Is this whole neighborhood haunted?

As soon as the thought crossed her mind, the bulletin board on her wall began to vibrate. Her basketball tournament medals shook as they banged against each other.

Treva walked to the bulletin board to stop the noise and held out her hand to touch it. The second her fingers met the board, the trembling stopped. She looked around her room for any sign of a ghostly visitor and didn't see anyone.

Is someone in the room with me? She felt as if she were being watched.

Just then, her bedside lamp illuminated. It stayed at the dimmest brightness for a second, then lit up brighter, then the brightest before going dark again.

Before Treva could react, it cycled through the light three more times, right before her eyes.

She couldn't see any hands, ghostly or otherwise, touching the base of her lamp.

Just like in the hallway earlier in the afternoon, Treva felt a distinct chill in the air. It felt like someone had left the freezer door to their refrigerator open, letting the iciness inside spill out.

I'm not alone, Treva realized, feeling as if she were on the verge of screaming. Her mouth was open and ready, but something inside held her back. She went to the dark lamp and touched the base again to light it up.

As she did, the skin on her hand turned goose bumped. The dim light lit the corners of her room. Standing there in the corner was a young woman who looked to be about three years older than Treva. She stood, watching her from the space between Treva's closet and her dresser. The young woman's eyes seemed empty and distant, as if they could see her but were looking right through her. The woman's mouth hung open as if she was silently groaning.

Treva backed up against the wall, kicking her basketball accidentally, knocking it across the room.

"Please leave me alone," Treva whispered. Her voice

felt small and wavered as fear sent shivers through her body.

The woman's face didn't change, and Treva felt almost certain she was going to lunge at her like the old woman outside of Cheesy Jerry's. Waves of cold washed over her, and she felt a nervous sweat form on her forehead. She closed her eyes, hoping to block out the woman from her sight and mind.

Let this be a nightmare, Treva thought. *Please let me just be asleep.*

When she opened her eyes, she saw the woman backing up toward the door. As soon as her body touched the doorframe, she began to fade.

In a matter of seconds, the ghost woman had completely vanished.

Treva stood, pressed up against the wall, illuminated only by the lowest setting of her lamp. She could hear her breath coming in ragged, as if she'd just run a series of sprinting drills on the basketball court.

"We have to move," she whispered to the silence.

CHAPTER 6

UNLUCKY ONES

It took everything Treva had to take a step toward her bedroom door. She stood against the wall for what felt like hours, afraid the woman was going to appear in front of her again. After she'd somehow convinced herself it was safe to move, she walked carefully across her bedroom floor, watching for anything paranormal.

One of the floorboards beneath her feet creaked, nearly giving Treva a heart attack. The next step made her kick her basketball, and she cried out, certain that something beneath her bed had grabbed her bare foot. The ball rolled harmlessly against the bookshelf, making one of the basketball trophies on top of it wobble slightly.

Treva froze, listening for any noise, ghostly or otherwise. The apartment was silent. Outside, a car drove quietly past the apartment building.

She continued but then stopped again, just inside the doorway leading to the hallway. After taking a deep breath, she peered down the hallway toward the bathroom and living room. Both rooms were dark and quiet. To be sure the coast was clear, Treva waited another moment, half expecting the woman was going to appear in the darkness and come back her way.

Straining to find anything unexplainable in their apartment, her eyes played tricks on her, making her see shapes and faces in the dark. She took a deep breath, closed her eyes for a moment, and opened them again.

The woman wasn't there, or at least not anywhere that Treva could see from where she stood.

With a resolute breath, she stepped across the hallway and pushed open the door to her dad's bedroom. The metal-on-metal squeak of the old hinges made her cringe and check the hallway again. She didn't want to alert the ghost to where she was.

We live in a haunted house, Treva thought. *Apartment, whatever.*

Thinking she'd find safety with her dad around, Treva stepped in. Her lamp across the hall cast enough light so she could see him sacked out on his back. His mouth was open, as if he were belting out a silent opera tune into the night.

She reached and touched his toes through the thin blanket that covered him.

"Dad," Treva whispered. "Dad, wake up."

Her dad snorted for a moment, and then he made a chewing sound with his mouth, as if she'd interrupted a meal he was dreaming about. After another few foot shakes, he groaned.

"Treva?" His whisper sounded faint and strained. It sounded like he was coming out of hibernation.

Treva didn't mess around. She continued to the side of his bed and stood there, arms crossed in front of her. It was then she realized she still felt cold from her ghostly encounter.

"There's a ghost in our house," Treva whispered. "We have to get out of here."

"What?" Dad asked. "What are you talking about? Did you say a ghost?"

Treva watched as her dad sat up in bed and rubbed one of his eyes with a bent pointer finger. He squinted, like the dim light was too bright and he was still trying to get his bearings.

"There was a woman in my room, watching me," Treva said.

Before he could respond, she reached over to her dad's bedside lamp and turned it on. Dad winced as light was cast into all corners of the room. Treva looked

to see if the woman had followed her there and might be watching them from one of the walls.

"Okay, okay," Dad said, exhaling in exhaustion. "Give me a second here, would you?"

Treva turned and watched the doorway, almost certain she was going to see a face peeking around the doorframe at her and her sleepy father. Part of her almost hoped that the light in her own bedroom would turn off and on like it had when the ghost was in there with her. Treva could point to it for proof.

She watched it and the hallway for a moment, but nothing happened.

"Did you say you think you saw a ghost?" Dad asked, his eyes finally adjusting to the light. "Here? In our apartment?"

Treva turned back to her dad and nodded.

"I've seen a whole bunch of them since we've moved here," Treva admitted.

"In our apartment?"

"Well," Treva reasoned, "no. I've seen most of them in the park. I even saw one at work yesterday. There was a man outside earlier tonight, and then the woman was in my room."

Dad didn't say anything, but Treva could see he was taking it all in, thinking about it. He threw back his blankets and climbed out of bed with a groan.

"Ugh," he muttered. "I'm still sore. Remind me not to move again anytime soon, okay?"

Treva nodded and stepped back as her dad walked around the side of the bed and toward the doorway. He paused in the hallway and glanced toward the living room and kitchen. Seemingly satisfied, he continued into Treva's bedroom.

Treva followed her dad, also looking down the hallway for a sign of anything spooky. She quickly joined him in her room and pointed to where she had seen the ghost.

"She made stuff shake in here too, like there was an earthquake or something," Treva added. "Then she made the light go off and on a bunch of times."

"Weird," Dad said, looking around. "You don't just think you saw a shadow from outside or something?"

"No," Treva said, shaking her head. "The light was on, and that wouldn't explain why the lamp went crazy."

Dad shrugged. "Those touch lamps are weird," he reasoned. "Maybe there was a power surge or something."

Treva sighed.

"You don't believe me," she said, struggling to hide the disappointment in her voice.

"That's not it at all," Dad said. "I'm just trying to find an explanation, that's all."

Treva sat down on the bed. She could totally see every "ghost" in her mind, clear as day.

"Look," Dad said. "We've been through a lot in the last few months, and—"

"Dad, I know what I saw!" Treva yelled, perhaps a little too loudly for the time of night.

Her dad nodded and put up his hands to show he didn't want to argue about it.

"I believe you, okay?" Dad said. "I really do. I'm just trying to wrap my head around what you're seeing. It's not every night you're awoken from a deep sleep to try and figure out if your new apartment is haunted. I'm adjusting."

"It's not just our apartment," Treva said. "I think we need to move."

Dad blew the air out of his lungs as if he'd taken a shot in the stomach.

"Let's slow down," he said. "We're not moving anywhere, Treva, okay?"

"There are ghosts in this neighborhood, Dad," Treva cried.

She cringed, wondering if the ghost woman or anything else dead within earshot had heard what she said. The last thing she needed to do was anger the spirits that seemed to be coming out of the woodwork.

"We don't know that for sure," Dad said. Treva could tell he was trying to pick his words carefully.

"I'm not the only one who sees them," Treva said. "A girl I play basketball with can see them too. She just doesn't want to talk about it."

Dad nodded. "But she's okay? Like, they haven't hurt her or anything?"

Treva thought about that. "No? I don't know," she admitted. "She's not the friendliest person I've met since we've moved in."

"So if they're real—"

"They are real," Treva corrected.

"All right. So it doesn't sound like these ghosts are looking to cause any harm," Dad said. "Maybe they're just hanging around or something, unsure they're even dead."

Treva shuddered.

"That's the creepiest thing I think you've ever said," Treva said.

She glanced over her shoulder as if something had put a hand there.

"The best thing you can do is ignore them," Dad said. "I have a feeling that they'll just go away."

Treva took a deep breath and sighed internally.

How was she supposed to sleep and live in a place where the dead just seemed to think it was okay to drop by?

"Can you at least try?" Dad said. His face looked concerned, like maybe he thought his own daughter was losing it.

"Yeah," Treva said. "I can try."

She thought for a moment, and a question tumbled out of her mouth before she could stop it.

"Do you think Mom might be a ghost?" Treva asked quietly.

Her dad was quiet for a moment, as if he was really thinking about it.

"I don't think so," Dad said. "I think Mom went to the best place possible."

Treva nodded.

"Yeah," she said. "I do too."

———————

The next morning, after a rough night of sleep, Treva made a decision. She wasn't going to let her fear of ghosts keep her from living her life. After a quick breakfast of waffles and some orange juice, she decided to throw the basketball around a little before work at ten.

As she dribbled the ball down the sidewalk, Treva

glanced at the people walking around outside. She tried not to worry if there were dead people mingling in with the living. The words Des had said the day before kept ringing in her head.

You'd best ignore them, New Girl.

And so Treva did.

As she approached the park, she saw it was mostly empty, save for one familiar face. Unsure how welcome she'd be, Treva tried anyway.

"Okay, seriously," Treva called. "Do you live here or something?"

Des caught her own rebound and looked Treva's way.

"I could say the same about you, NG," Des said.

"NG?" Treva said, confused. "Oh, right. New Girl. Nice."

Des didn't seem any more friendly than she had been when they'd first met, so Treva took the empty court to shoot her own baskets. She practiced her jump shot, finding her range from different spots on the painted pavement.

She stopped and stole a glance at Des, who kept taking free throw after free throw and sinking them. Treva almost applauded but figured that would anger Des. As Treva turned back to practice, she caught the image of a faded teenage boy standing near the corner of the park building.

He was tall and skinny and looked at the courts with a blank stare in his empty eyes. His clothes were old and worn, as if he'd done plenty of work in them. It didn't take Treva long to realize he was yet another ghost in a neighborhood that was seemingly full of them.

Look away, look away, Treva warned herself. She could feel her heart beat faster and her instinct to run kick in. Despite it, she held her ground and concentrated on her basketball. She knew that if she kept her eyes where they belonged, the boy would fade away like all of the others had.

Treva put up another shot, but it went wild, a little to the right, and dropped. She hustled and grabbed the ball, dribbled three times, and then glanced up.

The ghost boy nodded and put his hands up as if someone had yelled at him. He slowly turned and walked around the corner of the building, slowly fading away to nothing as he did. Treva turned to see Des looking in the ghost's direction and muttering something.

"Wait a second," Treva said. "Did you just talk to that ghost?"

Des struggled for a moment, as if she was trying to find something snappy to say in return. Instead, she just shook her head and threw the ball up in front of her, giving it some backspin.

"I don't know what you're talking about," Des said.

"Okay, seriously? You need to come clean," Treva said. "There are spirits wandering around pretty much everywhere, and you're acting like you don't care."

She held onto her own ball and walked onto Des's court.

"You're right, I don't care," Des said. "I just want to live my life—is that so wrong?"

Treva just pointed at herself. "So do I," she cried. "But I see them pretty much everywhere I go. I had one in my bedroom last night."

Des cleared her throat and looked elsewhere. To Treva, it seemed like Des didn't want to look her in the eye.

"Well, then you and I are the unlucky ones," Des replied. "Not everyone can see them."

"But you can hear what they're saying?" Treva asked. "As well as see them?"

Des nodded slowly as if she didn't want to admit it.

"Yeah," Des said. "I guess so."

Treva dropped the ball and let it roll over near the fence.

"How are you doing that?" Treva asked. "I've only been able to see them."

Des took a deep breath.

"We shouldn't even be talking about this," she whispered. "This is only going to make things worse for the two of us."

"Please," Treva said. "I need to know. I'm scared to sleep in my own bed."

"I just sort of opened myself up to talking to them," Des said. "But I wish I hadn't."

"You opened yourself up?" Treva asked. "What does that even mean?"

"I don't really know how to explain it," Des said. "Look, I warned you to ignore them. If they know you can see them and talk to them, it's . . ." Des trailed off as if she didn't want to finish that thought.

"It's happening to you too," Treva said.

"Not at my place," Des said. "But anytime I'm here. If I concentrate and don't think about them during a game, they just sort of back off. When I'm alone, they tend to show up more often."

Treva considered what she'd just learned. It made sense that Des was so intense during their games. Not only did she want to win, she wanted to keep the ghosts at bay.

"What did you say to that one that was just here?" Treva asked.

"I told him to get lost," Des said. "But it doesn't matter."

"Why not?"

Des looked Treva right in the eye and smirked.

"Because he'll be back," she said. "They always come back."

CHAPTER 7

DIGGING DEEP

Treva punched in at Cheesy Jerry's a few minutes before her shift. She was hopeful that working for a few hours would help keep her mind occupied. The last thing she wanted to do was stare at everyone she saw walking up and down the streets of her neighborhood to see if they were a ghost.

"I'm glad you're here, T," Frank said. "We're getting creamed!"

He wiped his hands on a towel before expertly tossing it into a laundry bin.

"Okay," Treva said. "What do you need?"

"Rolls," Frank said, pointing to the back storage room. "As many bundles as you can bring."

Treva hustled, bringing the workers in the kitchen whatever they needed, making sure they had all the necessary supplies to keep making more of CJ's world-famous steak sandwiches. The smell of onions grilling made her eyes sting, but she got used to it in time. When the end of her shift came and went, Treva kept working.

"Can you stick around?" Ronny asked. "We could use you. The outside looks like a bomb went off."

"Of course," Treva said.

The lunch rush gave way to an even busier after-lunch rush. Treva found herself changing garbage liners, wiping down tables, and making sure the napkin and condiment areas were well stocked. Ronny and Frank had her bouncing between tidying the outside and being a runner for things they needed inside.

During that time, Treva did her best not to think about the ghosts in her neighborhood. Despite how abrasive Des had been the few times she'd spoken to her, the girl did have a good strategy for dealing with the wandering spirits.

Don't pay any attention to them and they'll go away.

She was sweeping the space beneath a few of the empty picnic tables, dragging bread crumbs and bits of wrapper into a pile. As she cleared the last of the litter from beneath a table, she looked up.

Across the street was the old woman she'd seen while working her first day. She stood near another building that Cheesy Jerry's owned. The space was used to sell company T-shirts and souvenirs. The woman was hunched over, watching Treva from afar. Though

Treva felt her own pulse quicken, she looked down and pretended that there was nothing out of the ordinary.

Out of sight, out of mind, she said to herself, sweeping the piles into the dustbin.

When she looked up again, she could see the woman was still staring at her.

"Don't look," Treva whispered to herself with a scolding tone. "She's not really there."

As she turned, an older guy with a head full of silver hair stopped at the nearby garbage can and smiled at Treva.

"You're seeing one of them, aren't you?" the man asked.

The man's teeth were a yellowish gray, and one of the teeth in the front was a darker color, as if it were dead but still hanging around in his mouth. He had a rough complexion, looking like someone had walked on his face with cleats.

"I'm not sure what you're talking about," she lied.

Treva realized she sounded a lot like Des. More than anything, she wanted to pretend the ghost across the street and the ones in the park didn't exist.

If I pretend they're not there, then they're not.

The man set his orange tray in the space above the

garbage can set aside for tray returns. He acted like he hadn't heard a thing she said.

"I used to see them too," the man said. He was looking out at a different part of the block, making her realize he really couldn't see the ghost.

Treva couldn't keep up the act. Instead, she was intrigued by what he had to say.

"You don't see them anymore?" Treva asked, her voice coming in a hushed whisper.

"No," he said, almost wistfully. "I think they realized I couldn't do anything for them, and they just sort of faded away."

Do anything for them? Treva wondered. What did that even mean? What could anyone living do for the dead?

Glancing at the window to make sure Ronny wasn't watching her, Treva set her broom aside. Frank and Ronny didn't seem to need anything, and it wouldn't kill them if she took a break to find out more.

"What's going on with this place?" Treva asked. "Why are they here?"

The man shook his head and raised his eyebrows slightly as if thinking about what she'd just asked him.

"Nasty business from the past," the man said.

He scratched the back of his head with his giant

hands, then wiped the corner of his mouth with the top of his wrist.

"Tell me," Treva pleaded. "I moved into this neighborhood a few days ago, and I've seen the people that just aren't . . ." She trailed off, not wanting to say what she was really thinking.

"Ghosts, you mean?" the man said.

"Well, yeah," Treva said. "I figured out they were ghosts. I never really believed in them before. Now they're everywhere."

The man looked uncomfortable suddenly, which made Treva think she'd said too much already.

"I'd tell you, but you'd never be able to sleep again," the man said.

Treva held her ground. "Please," she pleaded. "I'm fifteen, not some eight-year-old who gets nightmares or something."

A couple of older men farther down the sidewalk called out the name "Peter," making the man look away from Treva and wave. He took a few steps toward them before she spoke up.

"Wait!" she said.

"Look, kid," Peter said, "I shouldn't have said anything. It's not my place, and it's not my business."

"I need to know what happened," Treva said. "You have to—"

"If you dig deep enough, you'll discover the truth about this place," Peter said. "But just remember that I warned you."

And with that, the man walked away from Cheesy Jerry's, leaving Treva standing near the bright-orange picnic tables, wondering what he could possibly mean.

———————

That night, Treva ate dinner alone while her dad was at work. When she finished, she cleaned up the kitchen and went into her room. There were murmurs from the neighboring apartments and creaks in the floor. Anytime she felt a little frightened, she reminded herself to focus and not think about what may or may not be in the apartment with her.

Stay busy, Treva said to herself. *No matter what. If you're busy, you don't have time to think about what's around you.*

The sun started to set, casting an orange glow across Capitolo Playground. She could see that there were people playing basketball, but she couldn't tell if they were her teammates from before or a bunch of older kids.

Instead, she fished her tablet from her backpack

and tapped on a web browser app. After a second, the search window came up. She thought about what the old guy, Peter, had said at CJ's earlier.

What could have possibly happened here in this neighborhood? she wondered.

Not sure where to start, she typed in "PASSYUNK SQUARE TRAGEDY."

A bunch of articles that didn't have anything to do with something awful happening popped up. Treva scanned some of them, looking for any sort of "nasty business" that might have contributed to the ghost population in her neighborhood.

There was nothing.

She cleared the field and typed "OLD PASSYUNK SQUARE."

A series of wiki articles about the history of the neighborhood was displayed, along with some pictures from around the community, some maps, and a listing of previous businesses. Treva scrolled through those too. Nothing seemed to jump out at her. As she moved back up to the search window, one of the maps caught her eye.

"Hello there," Treva whispered. "What's this?"

She tapped the picture, and a map opened, showing

an old map of South Philadelphia from the 1940s. She looked at it, trying to figure out where her apartment building might be. She zoomed in, finding familiar main streets that likely hadn't changed in decades. Since a lot of the streets didn't have the same names back then, it was hard for her to frame up what belonged where.

To make it easier, she opened up another tab and found a current map of the city. She saved both the old map and the new one in an image-editing application and opened the old map. She took the current map and changed the transparency to 50 percent. With her finger, she was able to drag the more current map of Philadelphia over the older map.

"How am I supposed to line this up?"

She thought about which structures would have been standing in the 1940s and which would still be standing today.

"Liberty Bell," Treva whispered aloud. "Independence Hall."

Within minutes, she was able to locate both on the maps and line them up. Knowing her neighborhood was just south of the historic landmark, she located her neighborhood on the old map.

With a little work, she found the area where Cheesy

Jerry's would someday be built. When she looked to the west, she expected to find Capitolo Playground.

It wasn't there.

What she found instead took her breath away.

She zoomed in to where the park was supposed to be on the map. Instead of the words CAPITOLO PLAYGROUND, she found the words LAFAYETTE CEMETERY.

Treva gulped. *I think I dug deep enough.*

CHAPTER 8

OLD TRUTH

"What the heck?" Treva whispered, staring at the screen. "There used to be a graveyard where the park is?"

Treva could feel her heart thrum a little more quickly knowing she had uncovered something important. Her finger hovered over the web browser app, pausing. She wasn't sure she wanted to know more.

Nasty business from the past.

The words Peter had said outside of CJ's repeated themselves in her head. She could see his friendly face and oddly colored teeth as if she were standing on the sidewalk, talking to him again.

"What didn't you want to tell me?" Treva whispered.

She opened up the search window and typed in "LAFAYETTE CEMETERY." A series of articles about cemeteries that also happened to be named *Lafayette* popped up. Treva scrolled through entries for the very famous cemetery in New Orleans. She caught glimpses of the strange above-ground tombs and vaults the bodies were stored in.

"Focus, Treva," she told herself.

She backed out of articles that had nothing to do with what she was looking for. To make her search more refined, she added "PA" behind "LAFAYETTE CEMETERY," and a small number of results popped up.

Treva opened them up one by one.

What she read completely blew her mind.

———————

Treva didn't sleep well after having learned that Capitolo Playground was built on top of a former cemetery. Even so, when morning hit, she knew she had to tell Des what she'd discovered.

After a quick breakfast, she changed and went out to the park, not even bothering to bring her basketball. The entire playground was empty; it was much too early for anyone in the neighborhood to even consider shooting hoops or kicking the soccer ball around.

She scanned the horizon, looking for any sign of Des heading out to play. Surprisingly, she didn't even see a ghost out in the morning light, staring blankly back at her. It blew her mind that there had once been gravestones where kids were playing sports and swinging on swings.

A shiver ran up both of Treva's arms, despite the warm summer weather.

It's too early for Des to be out, she thought, and started to head back home. At the very least, she could tell her dad what she'd discovered. Maybe that would be enough to get him to move.

As she passed through the opening in the fence along 10th Street, she saw a familiar face. Des was walking down the street, carrying a plastic sack full of groceries. She was in her own world, listening to music with her earbuds in and softly singing along.

Remembering it wasn't a good idea to sneak up on Des, Treva cut across the street and doubled back so that she was approaching her basketball rival head-on.

Des looked up and saw Treva on the sidewalk. Immediately, her face changed.

"Oh, come on," Des said. "You're stalking me now?"

Treva waited until Des turned off her music and pulled her earbuds out.

"I need to tell you something," she said. "And you're not going to believe it."

Des shook her head.

"Well, you're going to have to tell me walking, New Girl," Des said. "I need to get breakfast back home or my brothers will flip. I'm stuck watching my little brothers all day."

Treva shrugged. "That works."

As they started walking, Treva found the best place to begin.

"You know where we play basketball? Capitolo Playground?"

"You mean the spot where you and your crew are consistently embarrassed by mine?" Des said. "Sure, yeah, I know the place."

Treva braced herself for Des's reaction to what she was about to say next.

"Well, up until around 1946, it used to be a graveyard," Treva said.

"Huh?" Des asked, stopping at the corner.

Treva stopped too.

"There was a huge, run-down old graveyard where the park now sits," Treva said. "The city saw the cemetery as valuable real estate and had someone come and dig up the bodies to move them to different cemeteries."

Des breathed a sigh of relief. "Well, good," she said. "No more bodies under my court."

Treva cleared her throat and shook her head.

"Yeah, well, that's the problem," Treva said.

"No, no," Des said. "There's not a problem. C'mon, New Girl. There doesn't have to be a problem."

"The thing is, there were forty-seven thousand bodies in Lafayette Cemetery," Treva said, nodding toward the park. "And people say there's no way they got them all out of there."

Des closed her eyes for a long blink and tilted her head to the sky.

"So we're playing basketball on top of forgotten dead people? Is that what you're telling me?"

Treva nodded. "Yeah," she said. "I think so."

Des opened her eyes and looked over at the park. "So where'd they put the people they did pull out of the ground?"

"I guess they were supposed to put a bunch of them into a cemetery in Bensalem, but even that got screwed up," Treva explained. "The guy who was in charge of relocating the dead dumped them in a mass grave."

"Like in a pile?"

"Yeah," Treva replied quietly. "I guess that's one way to put it. He was supposed to give them new grave markers, caskets, everything. That didn't happen."

"That's completely messed up," Des said, and whistled through her teeth. "No wonder we're seeing ghosts."

The two of them stood there in silence for a moment as if taking all of the information in.

"I think we need to do something about it," Treva said.

Des shook her head. "Oh no," she said. "If you think we're going to dig up these people and give them a property burial, you've—"

"No," Treva replied, cutting her off. "There's no way we can do that. I think we need to try and talk to them."

"What?"

"Yeah," Treva said. "You can hear them. Maybe we can find out what they want and how we can help them or something."

She braced herself for the verbal onslaught she was almost certain was coming. Des was going to call her idea ridiculous and make some sort of crack about how she was crazy, and why wouldn't she just leave her alone already.

Des didn't do any of that.

"I knew I didn't like you from the start," Des said, her face twisted into a half smile. "You just don't know when to leave things alone, do you?"

"Yeah?" Treva replied. "Maybe not, but you don't live across the street from a paved-over graveyard."

Des nodded to a brick apartment building with a white-and-black striped awning. Two little boys were watching them from the steps.

"Close enough," Des said.

A quiet moment passed between the two girls. Treva didn't know if anything would come from her plan but figured it was worth a shot.

"So you'll do it?" Treva asked.

"Yeah," Des said. "And maybe I'll regret it. Meet me in the park after the sun's gone down."

"Really?" Treva asked. "You want to do this at night?"

Des smiled. "Well, of course," she said. "That's when most of them come out."

At dusk, Treva started watching the window, looking for Des to show up. She began to doubt how good of an idea it was to sit in the middle of a park at night with ghosts wandering around and countless abandoned corpses below them.

What is this going to accomplish? Treva asked herself.

She'd gone back and forth in her head about how she knew they had to do something but wasn't sure what.

How could they fix something a shady property owner had done decades ago? There was no way to know which bodies were left beneath the park and which ones had been dumped into a massive pit.

But maybe the dead will speak to us, Treva thought. *Maybe we can find out why their spirits are still wandering around my neighborhood.*

It felt foreign to refer to Passyunk Square as "her" neighborhood, but Treva realized that's exactly what it was. She wasn't visiting. She lived here now.

She glanced up to see a flashlight moving back and forth in the middle of the soccer field. Though it was impossible to tell for sure, Treva felt pretty confident that it was Des trying to signal her.

Knowing Des could just as easily change her mind and call the whole thing off, Treva got up and scrambled out of her room to the front door.

"Where are you going?" her dad asked from the couch.

"Um," Treva said, trying to think of something clever. "I'm going to talk to dead people with Destiny Williams."

Her dad dropped the mini corn dog he was eating onto his plate.

"There's a lot to unpack there," he said, shaking

his head. "Have . . . fun? Don't stay out too late. Curfew starts soon."

"I'll be back in a little bit," Treva promised. "I'll just be across the street."

"Love you," Dad said.

"Love you back," Treva said as she closed the door behind her.

Good, she thought. *He just thinks I'm being a smart-mouth.*

"All right," Des said. "You're here. I was about to give up on you."

"Sorry," Treva said. "Didn't see your light until a few minutes ago. Where do we want to do this?"

Des looked around the park. There wasn't a ton of light in the middle of the soccer field, but there was a light along the side of the park's main building, plus residual light from CJ's across the street.

"The courts," Des said. "We want to be able to see who we're talking to."

The two of them set off across the field toward the empty, dimly lit courts. Treva knew that the park was intentionally dark at night, as they didn't want to encourage the city's youths to break curfew. Good thing she and Des didn't plan to be out long, and they certainly weren't planning to get into any trouble—at least she hoped not.

In a matter of moments, they were standing beneath one of the baskets. The netless hoop hovered above their heads like a metal halo.

"So, what do we do?" Treva asked, looking around.

Des shrugged. "I'm not really sure. I guess I could call for them or something."

The two of them looked out into the darkness, the void peppered here and there with the occasional head-lights or lights from the apartments on the other sides of the park.

"Hey," Des called. "If you're out there, we want to talk to you."

Treva felt a sudden chill, as if someone with really cold hands had touched the back of her neck. Her dad did that in the winter to show her how frigid his fingers were when he'd come in from shoveling snow.

They both kept quiet. Treva strained to hear over the sounds of people talking and eating at Cheesy Jerry's.

"Is it going to be too loud over here?" Treva asked.

"I don't think so," Des replied. "When they talk, I can hear them, no matter how loud it is."

Treva scanned the edge of the light, looking for any of the out-of-place ghosts she'd seen over the last few days. There didn't appear to be anyone out there, but she couldn't shake the feeling that they were being watched.

"Maybe this isn't a good idea," Treva said after another moment. "I guess they don't want to show up when—"

"There," Des whispered. She pointed to the walkway to the children's structure.

A woman and a man walked slowly toward Treva and Des, their dark, empty eyes staring into the two girls. Like the other ghosts Treva had seen, they looked

like they were dressed in old-world clothes, and they seemed faded and out of focus.

Here they come, Treva thought nervously.

CHAPTER 9

SPIRIT SPEAKERS

Treva turned and watched a cluster of ghostly children heading their way. She couldn't help but feel a spike of fear race down her spine. From the soccer field, an old woman in what looked like an antique white gown shuffled toward them.

Within a matter of moments, there were seven different ghosts standing at the edge of the basketball court, staring solemnly at Des and Treva.

"Well," Des whispered, her voice a little shaky. "They're here. What did you want to ask them?"

Treva took a shuddering breath, unsure what to do. For some reason, she thought Des would do all the talking, but that didn't appear to be the plan. She'd only ever told the ghost in her room to leave her alone.

And it worked.

"Hello," Treva whispered. Her voice felt small and frightened. "I'm not sure if you can hear me, but my name is Treva Gallo."

There was a pause. Treva looked and saw the ghost of the man move his mouth.

"They can hear you," Des whispered.

"You can hear him speak?" Treva whispered back. "They told you?"

"Yeah," Des said. "Keep going."

"You should introduce yourself too," Treva said.

"Shut up," Des said.

"It's kind of rude not to," Treva snapped back.

"Fine," Des said. "I'm Destiny Williams. My friends call me Des."

Treva watched as the ghosts seemed to take this new information in. The man's mouth moved again, and then the woman's.

"The dude's name is John, and his wife's name is Charlotte," Des said.

For some reason, knowing there were real names attached to the faded figures in front of them made Treva's stomach sink.

These were real people at one point, she thought. *Real people who passed on and were wronged in the afterlife by a careless group of people who took shortcuts with what should've been their final resting place.*

"Both of us can see you, and we want to help you,"

Treva said, biting back her fear as much as she could. "Why are you still here?"

Des covered her face as she listened to the voices that Treva couldn't hear.

"They're stuck," Des whispered. "They're unsure where to go."

"Stuck where?" Treva asked both the group of ghosts and Des. "Here?"

The ghost of the old man nodded; his sad, long face dipped to his chest as if he were completely miserable with where his soul had ended up.

"They're stuck under the park," Des said. "Just like you said."

Treva's mind swirled, and she thought of what it must be like for the ghosts. Stuck for decades in a place they didn't belong, unsure where to go and what to do. It sounded like complete torture.

"I'm sorry," Treva said. "I wish there was something we could do to help—"

"Oh wow," Des said. "Look."

Des pointed toward the open field. There were more spirits coming forward, heading their way. Men, women, and children of all ages. Some stopped farther back from the rest of the ghostly group as though they meant to hear what the two living girls in the park had to say.

Treva suddenly felt very overwhelmed.

What are we doing? she wondered. *What can we possibly do for these people of the past?*

"I don't like this anymore." Des sounded stressed. "They're everywhere."

Treva was feeling a little uncomfortable herself. She hadn't been sure what was going to happen if they

tried to talk to the ghosts, but she'd never expected to see almost twenty of them come forward in the dark.

How many ghosts are stuck here in the park?

She imagined the people responsible for moving the graves had missed a few, but were there more than that? Could there be hundreds? Thousands?

"Are they saying anything?" Treva asked.

"Oh yeah," Des said. "Over and over again, I hear 'take us away.' 'Get us out of this place.'"

Treva found herself taking a step back. She didn't want to appear scared of the ghosts, but she was very afraid.

"We don't know how," Treva admitted. "Tell us what to do!"

Des was turning around, looking at their surroundings. Though the ghosts didn't come any closer than the outskirts of the basketball court, Treva saw there were more and more souls joining the pack. Fear mixed with a sick feeling knotted her stomach.

Why didn't they leave the graveyard alone?

"They're not saying anything," Des whispered. "It's like they just went silent on us."

"Maybe they don't know how to fix their situation," Treva said. "I'll bet they're just as confused as we are."

Treva watched the ghosts staring back at them; their dark eyes seemed to see right through her body.

"What was the point of this anyway?" Des asked. She sounded both scared and irritated. "How did we think we were going to be able to help them?"

Seeing there were more of them than she'd ever thought, Treva realized there was nothing they could do. Scared and overwhelmed, she was about to tell them all to leave Des and her alone.

I can't do it, Treva realized, looking into their sad and forgotten faces. *I can't tell what's left of these people to hit the road and stop bothering us.*

"I don't know," Treva admitted. "Maybe tell them to go to the light or to let go?"

Des turned to the crowd of ghosts and started to open her mouth. Before she could get any words out, she shook her head.

"They can't," Des said. Her eyes were glistening as if she were being brought to tears. "They heard you and said they can't."

We've messed with something we shouldn't have, Treva thought. *We have no way of helping these people.*

Behind them, she heard a car approaching from the side street.

"It's the police," Des whispered. "We're not supposed to be out here this late. We should go."

Treva glanced over and saw the squad car too. As much as she hated to admit it, Des was right. They'd overstayed their welcome. The last thing they needed was to get in trouble for being in the park after curfew.

When she turned back around, every single one of the ghosts had disappeared.

"Wait," Treva whispered.

"Let's move," Des said. "C'mon."

Treva ran after Des into the darkness of the soccer field. As she did, she felt pockets of cold glance against her skin. It was as if the ghosts left behind a cold spot to mark where they stood. With every step, she felt tingles in her arms and neck.

She glanced back to see the police car continue past the empty basketball courts. She and Des didn't stop or turn on a light.

"Do you think we did anything?" Treva asked.

"Yeah," Des said. "I'm pretty sure we made it worse."

———————

To get them off the street, Treva unlocked the main entrance to her apartment building and let Des in. There was a mountain bike leaning against the wall and a bank of mail slots.

Des sat on the steps and rested her elbows on her knees.

"That was horrible," she said, shaking her head. Her braids swung back and forth as if they thought the plan was horrible too.

"I didn't realize there were so many," Treva admitted.

"And there could be a whole lot more," Des added. "Especially if what you read was true. Forty-seven thousand bodies? No way could anyone relocate that many dead people."

"I guess not," Treva said. "Not without leaving a bunch behind."

Des wiped her face with her hands and looked up at Treva.

"It's going to get worse for us now. You know that, right?"

Treva gulped. She thought she knew what Des meant.

"I told you the best thing to do was ignore them and they'd go away," Des said with a touch of anger in her voice. "It's like we've stirred the hornet's nest. Now even more of them know we can see and hear them."

Treva looked out through the glass door toward

the park. She half expected to see a few of the ghosts watching them from across the street. A wave of relief washed over her when she didn't see anyone.

"They're not going to leave us alone," Des said. "Our little town meeting out there is going to bring them out in droves."

Treva felt her stomach rumble, and she put a hand over it to try and settle it. She didn't know if it was just the sick feeling of disappointment, but she felt off.

"I wonder if there's more to all of this," Treva said. "Are they stuck here because their graves were disturbed?"

Des shrugged. "No idea," she said. "Maybe they're mad because their bodies were moved somewhere else."

That made Treva think of another possibility.

"Or maybe there were families that were buried together and now they're separated?"

Des whistled. "You really are kind of creepy, you know that? I got actual chills when you said that."

Treva smiled, despite how she felt. She watched as Des touched her own stomach as if she wasn't feeling all that well either.

Get us out of this place.

The words Des had heard and repeated to Treva rang

in her head again and again. Did the ghosts expect the two of them to dig up the graves and move them to a proper cemetery? There was no way that was going to happen.

"How are we supposed to get them out of the park?" Treva wondered aloud.

Des looked up. "Hold up a second. You're not talking about moving skeletons, are you?"

"No, no," Treva said, shuddering at the idea. "But they kept telling us they wanted to get out of this place. How do you nudge ghosts toward the light or the great beyond or wherever they're supposed to go?"

Des shook her head again. "No idea. It's not like there's a company that specializes in ghost removal."

Out of nowhere, a thought occurred to Treva.

"What if we went to the graveyard in Bensalem?"

"What?" Des asked. "Why would we do that?"

Treva shrugged. "I don't know," she admitted. "That's where the bodies were supposed to have gone. Maybe there are ghosts there that aren't at rest too."

"So you want to add more ghosts to our growing collection?" Des asked. "You don't think we have enough?"

Treva shook her head in frustration. "Maybe if you

talk to them, we can figure something out. It's a long shot."

"A really long shot," Des agreed. "I don't know."

Treva watched the girl on the steps, who seemed to be thinking it over. She prepared herself for the inevitable answer. Des already thought talking to the ghosts in the park had turned out to be a ridiculous idea. There was little chance she'd want to go.

"This is going to sound crazy," Des said, standing up. "But something inside me says we should make the trip."

Treva was floored. "Really? You sure it's not just an upset stomach?"

Des nodded. "Yeah, well, I've got that too," she said. "But maybe seeing that cemetery they were buried in will somehow connect the dots."

"Okay," Treva said. "Well, we just need to figure out how to get there and when."

"Tomorrow morning," Des replied quickly. "I'll have my older brother Marcus drive us. He just got his license. I'll convince him to do it."

"Really?"

"Yeah," Des said, heading toward the door. "Look up where we need to go, and we'll head out once he gets his butt up and out of bed. Come by around ten a.m. or so."

"Okay," Treva said.

Des paused for a moment. "Oh, and bring twenty bucks too."

Treva looked puzzled. "For what?"

"To convince my brother to give us a ride," Des replied.

CHAPTER 10

LAND OF THE LOST

The next morning, Treva woke up feeling awful. She opened her eyes and stared at the ceiling, wanting nothing more than to stay in bed. Her stomach felt full, and her head was heavy, as if it were filled with cement.

She picked up her phone and glanced at the time: 9:17 a.m.

Plenty of time to get ready for our trip to the cemetery, Treva thought.

She got dressed and ready for the day before coming into the kitchen. Her dad stood by the counter, studying the waffle maker.

"I can never tell when these things are done," he said, looking up for a moment.

"When the light is on, it's cooking," Treva said. "When it clicks off, it's done."

As if on cue, the light on the circular iron switched off.

"I knew there was a science to it," Dad said. "Your mom was a pro with this thing."

Treva nodded. "Yeah, she was."

Her mom had been a pro at a lot of things. She could fix computers, she ran marathons, and she could play just about anything on the piano after hearing it once.

Treva watched as her dad fished the waffle off the bumpy metal and tossed it onto a plate.

"You off to work today?" Dad asked, motioning for her to sit down and eat.

Treva sat and transferred the waffle to her own plate.

"No," she said. "I've got the day off. Got extra hours yesterday, though."

Her dad set the iron down on another puddle of batter and cursed under his breath as the tan mixture oozed from the sides.

"So, what are your plans?" he asked.

Treva paused, letting her fork hover above the waffle. Telling her dad she and Des were headed to a cemetery probably wasn't the best idea. He was going to think something was severely wrong with her.

"Just going to hang with Des a bit," Treva said.

"I'm glad you're making friends," Dad said. "I was

worried you weren't going to give this neighborhood a fair shake."

Friends *is an interesting word to describe us*, Treva thought. *More like partners in the paranormal.*

"Yeah," Treva said. "It's a strange place, but I'm trying to make the best of it."

She only ate a little of her waffle and sipped some of her orange juice. Her stomachache had killed her appetite, but she didn't want to say anything to her dad about it. The last thing she wanted was for him to worry.

"I'll see you in a bit," Treva said, giving him a quick hug before she headed out.

———————

Ten minutes later, Treva, Des, and Marcus were heading northeast on 95 to Bensalem. Treva sat in the back of the minivan, listening to the music that Marcus streamed through his phone.

"Skip this song," Des said. "It's making me sick."

"Driver controls the radio," Marcus replied. "Those are the rules, little sister."

"I can't turn sixteen soon enough," Des said, crossing her arms and looking out the window.

"Thanks for driving us," Treva said. "I know it's a

little weird . . ." She trailed off, not sure how to finish that sentence.

"Weird?" Marcus replied, glancing into the rearview mirror at Treva. "The only thing weird is why you two can't go to a mall closer to home."

Treva was about to say something, but Des turned and leaned in close.

"He doesn't know where we're going exactly," Des said. "And I found something else last night when I couldn't sleep. Give me your phone number."

Treva nodded but was confused. She reached over to Des's extended phone and typed her number in under the entry NEW GIRL. A moment later, her phone buzzed. When she opened the message from Des, she saw a link to an article. Curious, she clicked it.

A story opened up about how construction of the Neshaminy Shopping Mall in Bensalem had uncovered a surprising secret. Workers there had found a large number of bodies in the ground.

You've got to be kidding, Treva thought, working hard to hide her surprise.

She read on and learned that some of the bodies from Lafayette Cemetery had been buried there in a mass grave. Dumped in a pit and forgotten.

Treva saw Des looking back at her, shaking her head.

"It's a shame," she said solemnly. "I don't know how the people who did that could sleep at night."

"It's unbelievable," Treva admitted.

Treva noticed Des had her hand on her stomach.

"Are you still not feeling well?" Treva asked, leaning forward.

"My stomach feels like it's tied in a knot," Des admitted. "Other than that, I'm okay."

"Same here," Treva said. "My head feels a little off too."

She looked out the window as billboards and industrial parks whizzed by. The sun was out, and there were only a few clouds in the sky. It was a perfect day for playing basketball in the park and, she supposed, decent enough weather to visit a burial site.

"Almost there," Des said. "Hang a right here, Marc."

As they got closer, Marcus seemed confused.

"Did you give me the right directions?"

He leaned forward over his steering wheel to get a better view out of the windshield. There was nothing but green trees and open spaces.

"This is it," Des said. "Pull over here."

"There isn't a mall anywhere near here, D," Marcus said.

"Oh, that's later," Des replied.

Marcus mumbled under his breath, pulled over, and put the car into PARK. He sat in the front seat while Treva and Des got out. They stepped onto the grass and looked around. A warm wind blew past them, and a bird chirped in a nearby tree.

"Where do we start?" Des asked.

"I don't know," Treva admitted. "I was kind of hoping that—"

Before Treva could finish another word, she sensed a slight tug in her stomach. Her legs felt shaky, as if she might faint. Des looked like she was experiencing the same thing.

What's happening to us? Treva thought.

A second later, she felt a lightness throughout her entire body. It made her skin hum as if someone were lightly poking her with something sharp over and over. Treva could only describe it one way . . .

"I feel sparkly," she whispered.

"So do I," Des agreed.

Suddenly, Treva felt some of the sparkly sensation lighten. As if appearing out of thin air, the ghost of an older woman emerged from Treva's body, stepping out from her core and into the world. It was as if the ghost were passing through a door. Then another ghost followed. And another.

The same thing was happening to Des. One by one, a middle-aged man, a boy of about ten, and a woman in her early thirties stepped out of Des's body and onto the grass.

With every spirit that left her, Treva felt the heaviness in her stomach fade. When the seventh and last one moved away from her, she felt almost normal again.

"We brought them here," Treva whispered.

"I . . . I can't believe it," Des murmured, watching as the crowd of ghosts walked across the field.

As the ghosts moved across the cemetery, others appeared out of thin air. The passenger ghosts from Capitolo moved toward the ones in the cemetery. Some of the spirits embraced; others just stood in front of each other and nodded as if acknowledging their journey.

"They're reuniting," Des said. "Families and people torn apart when they moved their graves. Some look like they have reconnected with their remains. It's, it's . . ."

"Beautiful," Treva finished.

And just as quickly as the ghosts came together,

one by one, they faded away. While she had no idea how spirits and the afterlife worked, Treva liked to think that the ghosts, after decades of feeling trapped, were free to move on.

Treva felt a tear streak down her cheek. She looked over at Des and saw her paranormal partner was getting misty-eyed too.

A loud car honk behind them made Treva jump.

"Hey," Marcus shouted. "You two just going to stand there, staring at that field?"

Treva looked back at Marcus, then back at Des, who was laughing.

"He must not have seen anything," Treva said to Des. Des nodded.

"Nah," Des called to Marcus. "We're all done here."

———————

With some more bribing and another eight dollars, Marcus pulled over on a busy street across from Neshaminy Mall. Des pointed out the passenger side window.

"There!"

Marcus pointed the other way. "Okay, are you losing it? The mall is over there!"

Before he could even argue, both Treva and Des

scrambled out of the car, leaving the doors open. They ran to the small marker in the field and paused.

"Here we go again," Treva said.

She felt the familiar pull in her stomach as two more ghosts, a woman and a man who looked like a soldier, left her body. Three more emerged from Des. The two of them watched as the ghosts walked off into the field, greeted by other spirits who lingered on the land.

"My stomachache is gone," Des blurted. "I feel brand new."

Treva nodded. A feeling of being light and unburdened washed over her. It was almost like nothing could bother her anymore. She couldn't help but look up into the sun and smile.

She looked down at the granite marker. Affixed to its front was a metal plate with engraved words on it.

"You think that's all of them, Treva?" Des asked.

Treva looked at Des in shock. It was the first time since they'd met that she didn't call her "New Girl."

"Well?" Des asked. "Do you?"

Treva shook her head.

"Not by a long shot," she replied. "But it's a start."

———

Three days later, two girls were scrambling back and forth on one of the basketball courts at Capitolo Playground. They were battling it out in a fierce game of one-on-one, and both of them looked sweaty and worn out.

Even so, neither of them seemed ready to give up.

"What you got, T?" Destiny Williams shouted. Her arms were spread out, making her a true barrier to the basket.

Treva Gallo surged forward, faked to the left, and dribbled behind her back, duping Des for the moment. When her opponent lunged for the ball, Treva turned, leaving Des to swipe the empty air.

"Gotta be faster than that, D," Treva said. "Or you're never going to stop this!"

And before Des had any chance of getting to her, Treva executed one of her patented jump shots from the top of the key. The ball arced perfectly, dropping through the netless hoop with barely a sound.

"And, I think that's game," Treva said.

"I think you got lucky," Des said.

The two of them high-fived each other and went to the side of the court. Treva snatched up her water bottle and squirted what was left of its contents into her mouth. Des dragged a small towel across her forehead.

When Treva looked up, she saw two small kids watching them from the middle of the soccer field. They looked lost, confused, and from another time. Their dark eyes watched both of the girls carefully.

"Hi," Treva called. "Are you two lost?"

The little girl nodded her head slightly. Her even younger brother looked at her and did the same.

"What are your names?" Des asked.

The little kids mouthed something. To Treva, they sounded like tiny whispers in the wind. She still had a way to go, but she was getting better.

Des nodded.

"Greta and Albert? I'm Des, and this is Treva."

The kids dipped their heads as if they'd suddenly grown shy.

"Come with us," Treva said. "We'll get you to where you belong."

AUTHOR'S NOTE

I love a good mystery. Even more, I love uncovering something that people don't want to talk about. That seemed to be the case with the old Lafayette Cemetery in Philadelphia, the basis for the ghost story in this book.

I'd accidentally stumbled across the tale when digging into ghost stories for this book. Someone had offhandedly mentioned that a person had claimed that a ghost sat near him at a Philly cheesesteak restaurant. The ghost was a man with a bloody head who seemed out of place and confused. Doing a little more research, I discovered the truth about Lafayette Cemetery. The city wanted to turn the neglected chunk of land (and home to 47,000 dead people!) into a park. So they decided to move the cemetery.

The information about the circumstances for digging up and moving the bodies is true. No one knows for sure how many of the dead were left behind, just like no one knows for sure where all of the remains ended up. They were supposed to be moved to Evergreen Memorial Park (now Rosedale Memorial Cemetery) in Bensalem, but even then, they were just sort of dumped there. The plaque across the street from the mall is real, though; it memorializes the departed that were discovered there.

Cheesy Jerry's isn't a real place, but it's based on the world-famous Geno's Steaks restaurant in Philadelphia, which is located right across the street from Capitolo Playground. In fact, if you play basketball there, you're more than likely to smell the sandwiches across the street.

So if you ever end up in Philadelphia, be sure to stop by Geno's for a sandwich. Maybe even head across the street for a quick game of one-on-one. And if you happen to see a confused ghost or two wandering around the park, remember: they just want to find their way home.

ABOUT THE AUTHOR

Thomas Kingsley Troupe has been making up stories ever since he was in short pants. As an "adult," he's the author of a whole lot of books for kids. When he's not writing, he enjoys movies, biking, taking naps, and investigating ghosts as a member of the Twin Cities Paranormal Society. Raised in "Nordeast" Minneapolis, he now lives in Woodbury, Minnesota, with his awe-inspiring family.

ABOUT THE ILLUSTRATORS

Maggie Ivy is a freelance illustrator and artist who lives and works in the Ozark area in Arkansas. She found her love for art at an early age and pursued it with passion. She graduated from The Florence Academy of Art in 2010. She loves narrative elements and story-building moments, and seeks to implement them in her own work.

Eszter Szépvölgyi is a graphic designer and illustrator based in Budapest, Hungary.

DISCOVER MORE

HAUNTED STATES
of
AMERICA

BY THOMAS KINGSLEY TROUPE

A CALIFORNIA
GHOST STORY

A COLORADO
GHOST STORY

A FLORIDA
GHOST STORY

AN ILLINOIS
GHOST STORY

A LOUISIANA
GHOST STORY

A MINNESOTA
GHOST STORY

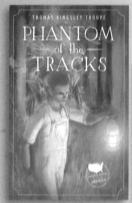

A NEW JERSEY
GHOST STORY

A TENNESSEE
GHOST STORY

A TEXAS
GHOST STORY